Would you rather be a Bullfrog?

By Theo. LeSieg

Illustrated by Roy McKie

COLLINS

Trademark of Random House, Inc., William Collins Sons & Co Ltd., Authorised User

ISBN (hardback) 0 00 171290-X

ISBN (paperback) 0 00 171280-2

© 1975 by Dr. Seuss and A. S. Geisel
Illustrations © 1975 by Random House Inc.
A Bright and Early Book For Beginning Beginners published
by arrangement with Random House Inc., New York, New York.
First published in Great Britain 1976
Printed & bound in Hong Kong

4 5 6 7 8 9 10

Tell me!

Would you rather be
a Dog . . . or be a Cat?

It's time for you
to think about
important things like that.

Would you
rather be
a Bullfrog . . .

. . . or be
a Butterfly?

Which one
would you rather be?
Come on, now.
Tell me why.

Tell me.
Would you rather be
a Minnow
or a Whale?

And tell me,
would you
rather be
a Hammer
or a Nail?

Would you
rather have
a Feather . . .

or a Bushy Tail behind?

Which would feel
the best on you?
Come on!
Make up your mind.

And . . .
would you rather be
a Cactus . . .

or a Toadstool . . .

or a Rose?

AND . . .
which would look
the best on you . . .

. . . the Long
or
Shortish Nose?

Would you
rather
be
a Skinny . . .

OR
would you rather be
a FAT?

Would you rather
be a Ball . . .

. . . or
would you
rather be
a Bat?

And once more
I'm going to ask you . . .
how about
that Dog and Cat?

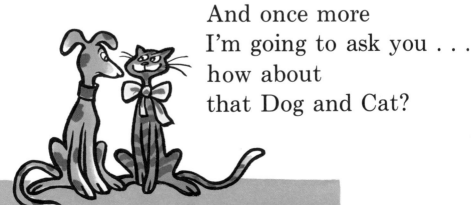

THINK, now!
Would you rather be

. . . a Rooster

. . . or a Hen?

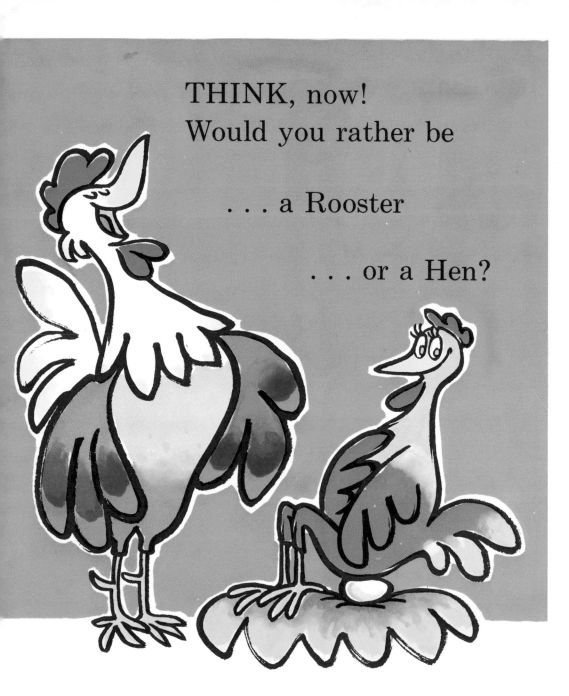

(How would you like to
lay an egg
every now and then?)

Would you
rather have
big Moose Horns . . .

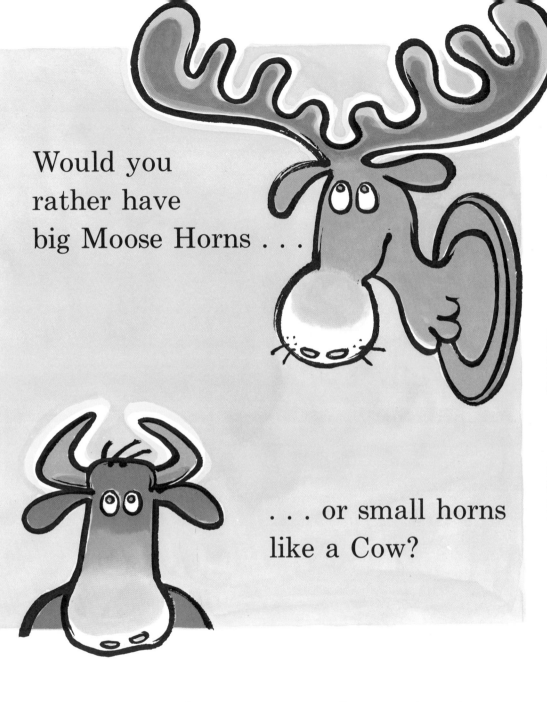

. . . or small horns
like a Cow?

This is so, so, so important
and I want
to know right now!

Would you
rather be
a Bloogle Bird
and fly around
and sing . . .

. . . or would you
rather be
a Bumble Bee
and fly around
and sting?

And tell me,
would you rather be
a Table . . . or a Chair?

And NOW tell me,
would you rather have
Green . . . or Purple Hair?

Would you rather be
a Clarinet . . .

. . . a Trombone

. . . or a Drum?

(How would you
like to have someone
going BOOM-BOOM
on your Tum?)

Suppose you had to be
a LETTER!
Well, then,
which one would you be?
Would you rather be a Curly one . . .

. . . like

. . . or

. . . or

Or would you rather
be a Sharpie . . .

. . . like

. . . or

. . . or

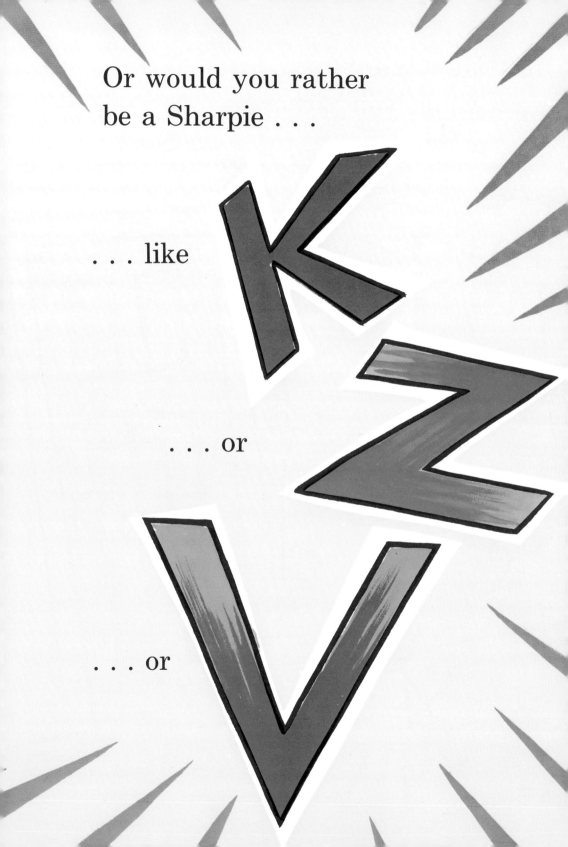

Now tell me . . .
would you rather be
a Window . . . or . . . a Door?

And would you
have more fun

if you had Six Feet . . .

or a Hundred and Sixty-four?

These are
real important questions.
Come on!
Tell me! Tell me please!

Would you
rather be
a Soda?

OR . . . .

A piece
of smelly
Cheese?

Would you rather
live in Igloos . . . or . . .
would you
rather live in Tents?

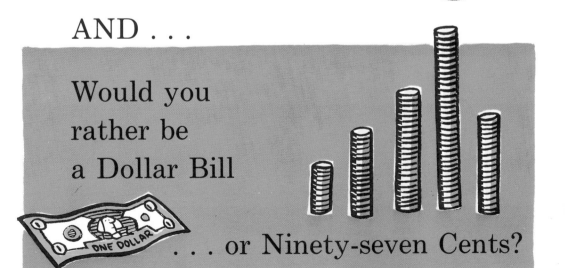

AND . . .

Would you
rather be
a Dollar Bill
. . . or Ninety-seven Cents?

AND would you rather be
a Mermaid
with a tail instead of feet . . . ?

OR . . .

Would you rather be
a Spook
and run around
dressed in a sheet?

Would you
rather be
a Jellyfish . . .

. . . a Sawfish . . .

. . . or Sardine?

AND
would
you
rather be
THIS Thing . . . or THAT . . .

or
the
Thing
that's
in between?

It's hard to make your mind up
about important things like that.

(I can't even make
MY mind up
about that
Dog and Cat.)